NO BORROWING, BRENDA!

NO BORROWING, BRENDA!

AND OTHER FAVORITE STORIES FROM HIGHLIGHTS
Compiled by the Editors
of
Highlights for Children

Compilation copyright © 1994 by Highlights for Children, Inc.
Contents copyright by Highlights for Children, Inc.
Published by Highlights for Children, Inc.
P.O. Box 18201
Columbus, Ohio 43218-0201
Printed in the United States of America

ISBN 0-87534-629-4

Highlights is a registered trademark of Highlights for Children, Inc.

CONTENTS

NO BORROWING, BRENDA!

By Kathleen Pestotnik

Brenda poured herself a second glass of juice and stretched her bare feet across the kitchen chair. It was not just any Friday. It was a no-school Friday. That meant she had the whole day to . . . uh-oh.

The scout meeting! She'd nearly forgotten, and it was her turn to bring treats. Brenda had promised homemade cookies. Her mom wouldn't be too happy about that. *Mom* had school today. She was the teacher half of parent-teacher conferences.

Just then, Brenda's mom hurried into the kitchen. "June will be here any minute to stay with you. And my conferences will be finished by noon at the latest. We can have lunch together. Anything you need before I go?"

"Could June and I bake this morning?" Brenda asked hopefully. "I have to take treats for Girl Scouts."

Her mom groaned. "I wish you had warned me. I'm out of everything."

"Mrs. Easton bakes a lot," Brenda said. "Maybe I could . . ."

"No borrowing, Brenda! Remember last time when you and June made gourmet fudge? I had to go to five stores to find that special brand of English walnuts you borrowed from Mrs. Easton."

The look on her mother's face as she grabbed her coat and hurried out the door warned Brenda not to argue with her.

"OK," Brenda said reluctantly. "No borrowing."

Now what? she wondered. She couldn't let the girls down. She dressed quickly and headed for the elevator. Maybe June would have an idea.

But when the elevator door opened, June was not there. The only passenger was hidden behind a huge armload of bulging grocery bags.

"Mrs. Easton? Is that you?" Brenda took the top

bag, and sure enough, Mrs. Easton's plump red face appeared.

"Bless you," she puffed. "I never . . . would have . . . made it . . . alone."

"You must be baking today."

"I wish I had time." Mrs. Easton sighed. "My grandchildren are coming, and they love home-made cookies."

Brenda set the bag in the doorway. "Have a good weekend," she called.

It wasn't fair, Brenda thought. Mrs. Easton wanted to bake but didn't have time. Brenda had the time, but . . .

"No borrowing, Brenda!" her conscience reminded her.

When June finally stepped out of the elevator, she was carrying two tennis racquets. "Hi, June. How come you have two racquets?"

"One for you and one for me, Brenda," June said, smiling and handing Brenda one of the racquets. "I thought I'd give you my old racquet because now I have this new one." She held the new silver and pink racquet near the window so its shiny metal surface reflected the sunlight.

"Where'd you get it?" Brenda asked admiringly.

"I traded for it—my old silver bracelet for this professional racquet. The girl who I got it from said she never liked to play tennis anyway." June grinned. "And since I have more bracelets than I can ever wear, I thought the trade was a pretty good deal."

A slow smile spread across Brenda's face. "Definitely a good deal for you, since you're playing on the tennis team at high school this year."

Brenda unlocked the apartment door. "Come on in. I've got to check something."

She took her mother's recipe box down from the kitchen shelf and found the card she wanted. One by one, she read off the ingredients and took them from their storage places, setting each item on the counter by the stove. Mom was right. They were out of sugar, eggs, and chocolate chips.

Brenda grabbed a pencil and pad from the drawer and figured rapidly. It just might work. She dug a paper bag out of the cupboard, pocketed her list, and started for the door.

June stared at her curiously. "Where are you going, Brenda?"

"Secret mission," Brenda replied mysteriously. "Don't worry. I won't leave the building."

She'd start with Mr. Landon. Mr. Landon lived alone, but he had a real sweet tooth. Then there was Mrs. Garcia and, of course, Mrs. Easton.

Brenda was back in five minutes. "Mission

accomplished," she announced, holding up the bulky bag. "Want to bake some cookies?"

"They don't call me Super Chef for nothing," June chuckled. "But are you sure your mom won't mind? Remember the last time . . ."

"It's OK," Brenda assured her. After all, it wasn't the baking her mom had objected to; it was the *borrowing*.

Ten minutes later the two were up to their elbows in sticky dough and the cookies were ready for the oven.

"We'd better stay right here and watch them," Brenda warned. "I want to end up with forty-eight perfect cookies."

It was almost noon when June flipped the last cookie onto the rack to cool. "Tasting time," she suggested.

Brenda shook her head. "Not yet." She took four plastic bags from the drawer and began counting cookies into them. Fourteen in the first bag, six in the second, eight in the third, and twelve in the last. She finished just as she heard her mother's key turn in the lock.

Brenda grinned sheepishly at her. "You're just in time, Mom."

Her mother sniffed the buttery-sweet aroma and frowned. "So I see. I thought we had an agreement."

"I didn't borrow. Honest!"

"Then how . . ."

"I *traded*. Mrs. Easton swapped her chocolate chips for a dozen cookies. Mr. Landon gets six in exchange for two eggs, and Mrs. Garcia . . ."

Her mom laughed. "I get the message. You found a way to bake without borrowing, and I don't have to make an extra trip to the store. I just hope you can break the news gently to your dad. Chocolate-chip cookies are his favorites, and you've traded them all away."

"Not exactly," Brenda said with a sly grin. "I made some for trading, some for treating, and some . . ."

"For eating!" they shouted together.

Satisfaction Guaranteed

By Alan Cliburn

Alex was all stretched out under a tree in his front yard when Dave walked past.

"Hey, where are you going?" Alex wanted to know.

"Looking for a job," Dave said.

Alex yawned. "Are you kidding? There aren't any jobs for kids our age. There's even a waiting list for kids who want paper routes."

"My dad says he'll get me a bike if I earn half the money for it," Dave explained.

"Sure, but I just told you—there are *no jobs* in this town!" Alex said. "You're new around here, but Harry and I went everywhere looking for work a few weeks ago."

"See you later," Dave said.

"Where are you going?" Alex asked.

"Looking for a job," Dave said.

"But I just told you—" Alex shook his head. "You'll find out."

When Dave reached the business district a few minutes later, he checked his appearance in the front window and then he walked right into Mitchell's Fine Furnishings.

"What can I do for you?" a man said.

"I'm looking for a job," Dave answered, swallowing. This was harder than he thought. "I could sweep the walk out front or empty the trash or—"

"Not interested," Mr. Mitchell interrupted. "I hired a kid about your age last summer. Very unreliable. And he did sloppy work, too."

Dave turned to leave, but then remembered something his father had once said: If things don't seem to be working out, try a different approach.

"I guarantee satisfaction, sir," Dave heard himself announce.

Mr. Mitchell gave him a look. "And just what does that mean?"

"It means if you aren't satisfied, you don't have to pay me," Dave explained.

"Well, I really don't know," Mr. Mitchell began.

"What have you got to lose?" Dave asked. "You open at nine o'clock. I'll be here at eight-thirty to sweep the walk. OK?"

"OK," Mr. Mitchell agreed.

Dave went up and down the boulevard, stopping at every store. Some people wouldn't even listen when they found out he wanted a job, but a few did.

The woman at Detwiler's Patio Restaurant repeated, "Satisfaction guaranteed?"

"That's right," Dave said.

"Well, this place is really a mess right after lunch," the woman admitted. "People leave their napkins and paper cups everywhere. I could use somebody to pick up around here after lunch—say, about two o'clock. But I'm afraid I couldn't pay you very much."

"I'll do it and I'll do a good job, too," Dave promised.

"The trash is picked up on Tuesdays and Fridays," Mr. Fogel of Fastprint Company explained. "But the alley is too narrow for that big trash truck. I have to take the cans down to the end of the alley. If I have a customer, it's hard for me to get away. But I need someone I can count on. Someone that is very reliable. I was thinking of getting a high school boy."

"I can do it," Dave interrupted.

"The truck comes around four o'clock," Mr. Fogel continued. "I like to get the cans down there by three-thirty in case it's early. Are you sure you can handle this?"

"I'm sure," Dave said. "And remember, if I don't, you don't have to pay me."

"Why, that's right," Mr. Fogel remembered, nodding. "Satisfaction guaranteed."

By four o'clock Dave had covered every store in town and had lined up five jobs.

Alex was still under the tree in his front yard as Dave headed home.

"I told you so," he called out. "You wasted all that time for nothing."

"I got five jobs," Dave replied.

"I don't believe it! How?"

Dave explained his "satisfaction guaranteed" policy.

Alex frowned. "You mean they don't have to pay if they don't like your work?"

"That's right," Dave said.

"But you could do all that work for nothing!" Alex exclaimed.

"Maybe," Dave admitted. "But at least they're giving me a chance. See you later."

"See you later," Alex echoed, shaking his head.

Dave was tired the next morning. That's one nice thing about summer, he thought. I can sleep as late as—suddenly he sat up in bed. He was due at Mitchell's Fine Furnishings at eight-thirty and it was already past eight!

"But I don't feel like sweeping the walk," he told himself.

"You promised," another voice seemed to say. "Get going!"

Dave arrived at the furniture store at exactly eight-thirty and began sweeping. It looked pretty good when he finished, but not so good as it might. He went over it again. Mr. Mitchell came out to inspect his work.

"Not bad," he said. "Keep it this clean and you've got a job."

It wasn't always easy, but Dave did the best he could on every job he had, even when it meant chasing napkins down the block after a windy lunch hour at Detwiler's Patio Restaurant.

He stuck with it, even on the really hot days when Alex and his other friends were going swimming. The money he earned didn't seem like much at first, considering all the work he had done, but he always put his money into the bank and in a few weeks was surprised by all the money he had managed to save.

By the end of the summer Dave had added a few more jobs, but he had no problem getting to them—not on his brand-new bicycle!

The Secret of the Evening News

By Mary Sherry

Karen stared at the blank paper on her desk. Then she sighed and gazed out the window. With another very loud sigh she leaned back in her chair and looked at the ceiling.

"Writing to Grandma and Grandpa is so hard!" she thought. "I can never think of anything to say."

"Well, I'll do it later," she said to herself, pushing the paper away. "It's too nice a day. I'll go outside for a while. Maybe I'll get some ideas later . . ."

"Finished so soon, Karen?" Mrs. Pearson called from the kitchen as she heard Karen come down the stairs.

"Oh, Mom! I can't think of anything to write!"

"Well, you know the deadline is tomorrow or no overnight at Lisa's. You have to learn to write your thank-yous promptly, and you're old enough to write a long letter while you're doing it." Mrs. Pearson's tone was very firm, and Karen could see her emphasize her firmness in the brisk way she was peeling potatoes for dinner.

"I know, I know. I'd have it done twenty times if I could think of something to write," Karen said.

"Just write your news," Mrs. Pearson suggested.

"News, news. I never have news."

"Of course you do, dear. You just have to think about the things you do as news."

At that moment the telephone rang. As her mom answered it, Karen ducked out the door into the bright afternoon, and she quickly forgot about writing her letter.

She came back inside just before dinner. Her dad was already home.

"How's Carefree Karen?" he asked, reaching up from the couch and giving her a hug.

"Oh, OK, I guess." Suddenly the excitement of the soccer game she had been playing wore off, and the nagging thought of the unwritten letter popped back into her mind.

"Hmmm." Mr. Pearson peered at her over his newspaper. "You don't sound so carefree to me. Anything you want to tell me about?"

"No, nothing special," Karen said.

"Well then, turn on the tv, and we'll watch the news."

Karen's mother joined them as they watched the report of the events of the day. The national and international report was about a new peace agreement. The next news item was about a special election in Ohio. Karen was very interested in the news from the state university about a new medicine that was expected to help a lot of people. The weather report promised rain and there were warnings of flooding in low areas. Finally, several sports experts gave their opinions about which baseball players would be traded this year. Their guesses prompted Karen and her mom and dad to make their own guesses.

As the news ended, Karen turned off the television set and went out to the kitchen.

"Did you listen to the program?" Karen's mother asked as she put the food into serving dishes.

"Yes," Karen answered, wondering if she should have noticed something special.

"Well, I hope *that* helps you write your letter." Karen's mom grinned at her with a challenging look.

All during dinner, they talked about what had happened at work, school, and home. Karen wondered all the while what her mom's strange smile had meant. How could the television news program help her write her letter? Her life wasn't as exciting as anything she heard on the news. Well, she supposed it was exciting to her and to her mom and dad, and, well, maybe it would be exciting to her grandparents, too.

Karen sat up suddenly. "May I be excused?"

Her parents exchanged glances. "Yes, you may. I guess we're finished," Mr. Pearson said.

"I'll be back to help in the kitchen," Karen called as she dashed for her room.

Back at her desk, she took a piece of paper and wrote:

1. National and International
2. Local
3. Weather
4. Sports

Then she took another piece of paper and began, Dear Grandma and Grandpa.

A little while later, Karen brought the letter—all four pages of it—into the kitchen and showed it to her mom.

"Karen! That's wonderful! Grandma and Grandpa will love it. Now tell me, how did you do it?" Her mom looked at her with a trace of that same grin that had mystified Karen before dinner.

"Well, I did what you told me. I thought of my life as the evening news." Karen showed her mother the list she had made. "Under National and International, I told Grandma and Grandpa what was happening at school and in the neighborhood. Under Local, I told them what was happening at home. Then I told them about our weather because ours is so different from theirs. And last I told them about my playing soccer for the first time this year. That's Sports."

Karen's mother gave her a hug that clearly said she was proud of her.

"But the best part, Mom, is that I don't think it will be hard for me to write letters ever again. From now on I will think of my life as news to the person who reads my letters."

"Good! And now that that problem is solved, let's get to the next one—dishes. You wash tonight."

"Oh, Mom!" Karen groaned. She took a glass from the sink and watched the water drip from it. Then she laughed. "If I wrote a letter about doing dishes, I know one thing for sure, it wouldn't come under Sports!"

The Snake That Played Possum

By Phyllis S. Yingling

Andy glanced up and down the street, sighed, and sat down on the porch steps. He could hardly wait for the Turners to come. They should be here any minute.

Andy tried to be patient. Camping! Wow! He had never slept overnight in a tent. But suppose it rained—suppose a snake crawled into the tent? What then? And how would he get along with Jeff's sister, Becky, who was deaf? Would they be able to understand each other?

"Come on, stop your worrying," Andy muttered to himself. "Everything will be fine."

Just then the Turners' station wagon pulled up, and Andy jumped down the steps and climbed into the backseat.

The state park where they camped was in the mountains about a two-hour drive from the city. It was a beautiful day. Wild flowers were everywhere, and birds darted among the bushes and trees. Becky had brought a friend along. Her name was Carole. She and Becky went to the same school, a special school for hearing-impaired children. Carole had never been camping before either, so she and Andy watched carefully and helped wherever possible as the others set up camp.

When the tents had been set up and the outdoor kitchen was made ready, Mrs. Turner said, "OK, gang, you've done a great job. Now go have some fun. Come back for lunch when all of you are hungry enough."

Andy could hardly believe it. What a neat place! There was a ranger station and nature museum and several trails leading to the woods and mountains.

Becky and Carole started along one trail and the boys followed. The girls talked constantly in sign language. Andy couldn't imagine how fingers could move so fast. Back at camp and in the car Andy had noticed that Mr. and Mrs. Turner and Jeff signed when they spoke so that Becky and Carole could be included in the conversation. When she was with the family, Becky used her voice, which was a little hard to get used to at first. But while talking to Carole, she used only signs.

"Wow," Andy said to Jeff. "I can't figure how they understand each other at all."

"Oh, you get used to it," replied Jeff. "Becky began using signs when she started school. I must have been about seven then. Some of her teachers came to our house to teach me and Mom and Dad so we could communicate with Becky. Believe me, it was hard. But we used it every day, so after a while it just came naturally to all of us."

The girls were running ahead now while the boys dawdled along the path. Jeff was looking for moths for his science project in school. Andy was trying to imagine how you could learn to talk if you couldn't hear what other people were talking about.

Just then, they heard a strange cry. The boys ran down the path. In a moment they rounded a bend and came upon the girls. Carole had tripped and fallen among some rocks and sat unmoving. Becky stood a few feet away from her, signing something. Among the rocks was a brownish gray snake, coiled, with its head and neck flattened like a cobra's.

Carole was frozen with fear.

Andy was scared stiff. He knew a cobra's bite could kill someone.

"OK, everybody," Jeff said calmly, putting his finger to his lips. "Just be quiet and stay still."

Andy didn't move a muscle, but he gasped as he saw his friend move stealthily over the rocks until he was behind the snake. Then, in a split second, Jeff reached down and grasped it just behind its head. He held it up in the air.

Andy wished Jeff would pick up a rock and bash the thing's head in. How could he stand there with it dangling from his hand? He didn't seem a bit afraid; he was grinning.

Then to Andy's horror, Jeff dropped the snake on the path in front of him. The snake rolled onto its back, its flat belly up, its mouth gaping.

Becky had helped Carole up, and the frightened girl stood trembling.

"It's a cobra, isn't it, Jeff?" asked Andy. "I mean, with the flat hood, it sure looks like one."

"No, it's a hognose. Couldn't hurt you if it wanted to. It's just an actor. See, it's only playing dead."

Carefully, Jeff flipped the snake over with the

toe of his boot. Immediately the snake flipped itself back into its belly-up position. "They're not poisonous at all," Jeff explained. "Acting is their only means of self-defense."

Becky was trying to explain to Carole that the snake was harmless, but it was clear by the fear in her eyes that she wasn't convinced.

Jeff leaned down and carefully picked up the unmoving snake. "Look at its nose. See how flat it is? That's why this snake is called a hognose. Easy to identify." Holding it toward Andy, he said, "You want to hold it?"

Andy didn't want to hold it. But he also didn't want to admit how scared he was, so he reached out his hand and grabbed the snake, as Jeff had, just below the head. The snake's body felt limp. Andy supported it with his other hand.

"See," said Jeff grinning, "that snake is more scared than you are."

Andy laughed. "You want to bet?" he asked. But now he could see the funny turned-up nose. It wasn't a cobra after all. He should have known. There aren't any cobras in the wild in the United States, only in zoos, sideshows, and occasionally as pets. Funny how frightened he'd been.

"Do you want to touch the snake?" Jeff signed to Carole.

Gingerly Carole reached out and touched its tail, then jerked her hand back and grinned sheepishly. "I don't like snakes," she signed. She didn't seem so afraid anymore.

Jeff took the snake from his friend and gently laid it in the dry leaves beside the path. Cautiously the snake moved its head from side to side, then slithered off into the bushes.

"That was some snake!" exclaimed Andy. "I could have sworn it was a cobra."

"Believe me, if it had been a cobra, I wouldn't have picked it up," said Jeff. "One thing our parents taught us when we started camping was to identify different kinds of snakes and not to fool around with poisonous ones. After lunch we'll go to the nature museum. They have all kinds of live snakes on display. They even have copperheads and rattlers in glass cages so you can learn to recognize them. They're the only kinds of poisonous snakes in this part of the country."

That night, as he lay in the pup tent, Andy thought about the day. His body was wonderfully tired after all the hiking and climbing. His mind was still full of the new things he had learned about snakes and rock climbing and how to identify wild flowers and birds. He had even picked up some of the signs the family used, and the girls had taught him how to fingerspell. Lying there in the dark, he practiced signing and finger spelling. "Goodnight," he said softly. "Goodnight, snake, wherever you are."

Muddy Millicent McNamara

By Mary Pratt

In the early spring Millicent McNamara collected dirt after school. But often it rained, so mostly she collected mud.

Collecting mud was easy. Millicent only needed a stick or a clam shell or an old rusty spoon to dig it up. She saved the mud in empty tin cans and jars.

Mud and dirt were everywhere she looked— under the pine trees in the backyard, beneath the front porch of the house, by the stream in the park. Mud was also in Millicent's hair, under her fingernails, and even in her ears.

Everyone in the family—Mom, Dad, her older brother, Jason, and Grandma McNamara—wondered what Millicent was up to. Digger, the dog, watched and wagged his tail.

"Millicent, why are you filling up those jars and cans with mud?" her father asked.

Millicent smiled. She did not have a reason for collecting mud—not yet. She would have to think of something soon, so she said, "It's a secret."

Jason said, "What a waste of time. I think I'm going to call you Muddy Millicent, Muddy Millicent McNamara." And he laughed and sputtered and coughed.

Millicent did not think it was *that* funny.

Then her mother said, "I think Millicent needs a good bath."

As she ran the water into the tub, Millicent said to herself, "Sometimes I'd rather be dirty."

The next day the whole family went to the park for the first picnic of the spring. Millicent took three large empty tin cans with her—just in case.

They had macaroni salad, cranberry relish, and Grandma's homemade bread. On the grill they cooked hot dogs, and for dessert they toasted marshmallows.

Finally, Mom asked, "Millicent, why did you bring those tin cans to the picnic?"

Millicent was worried. She still did not know what she would do with all the dirt and mud she was saving, so she said, "It's a special secret."

The sun had nearly set when Digger wandered down to the stream and began to paw at its bank. Millicent hurried after him.

On her way she saw the park's gardener pulling weeds from a bed of tulips. His hands were dirty and his boots were covered with mud.

By the stream Millicent collected more mud in her tin cans about as fast as Digger dug it up.

Then Dad said, "Time to go." He looked at Millicent and Digger and shook his head. "Time for another bath—for you *and* for Digger."

Millicent sighed. Was collecting mud worth all the extra baths she had to take? But Digger wagged his tail all the way home. He had found a large bone at the bottom of the hole in the stream bank.

Before Millicent went to sleep, Grandma came into her room. "What are you going to do with all that mud? I counted twelve cans and sixteen jars full of mud on the back porch."

Millicent still had not decided, but on the way home she had gotten an idea. "It's an extraspecial, very important secret. And I can't tell."

"Not even to your grandma?"

"Well . . . I'm sure you can keep a secret." Millicent whispered into Grandma's ear.

"What a perfectly wonderful idea, and it is the right time of year," Grandma said, and she kissed Millicent good-night.

The next day, Saturday, Millicent was up before anyone else. Quietly, she went to the garage and found several small packages inside a wooden box. Then she went outside and sprinkled something into each jar and tin can.

She waited. And waited. Then she waited longer and longer.

"Nothing's happened," she told Grandma on the third day.

"Just be patient—it will."

After eight days had passed, Millicent found something new in the jars and cans. "It worked! It worked!" she cried.

Everyone, including Digger, rushed outside.

"What do you think of my mud collection now?" Millicent brushed dirt from her jeans.

Mom looked into the jars. "They're full of little green sprouts."

"A tin-can garden. That's pretty clever," said Dad.

And Jason said, "I guess we can't call you Muddy Millicent any longer."

Grandma winked. But Mom said, "Not after you take another bath."

Millicent went inside. Dried mud spotted her shoes and dotted her nose. She had dirt in her hair, under her fingernails, and even in her ears.

But Millicent had another secret. Now that she was a gardener and gardeners were supposed to get dirty, she did not mind taking *baths*. Not at all.

The Winner's Ribbon

By Patricia L. Dombrink

It was perfect weather for an Independence Day parade. Usually the Fourth of July is hot and sticky, but today seemed just right. This is a good sign, I told myself. It means I'm going to win a ribbon in the parade.

I was thinking of this while I cleaned my boots. I was looking forward to marching with a group from our school. My sister, Michelle, had already dressed in her majorette's outfit. It was covered with sparkling red, white, and blue sequins, and her boots were high and white.

Just then Mom burst into our room. "Kids, I hate to do this," she began, "but I have to get to the hospital right away. They need another surgical nurse, and I'm the closest one available. One of you will have to stay with Grandpa."

Michelle and I looked at each other and groaned. I waved my red, white, and blue baseball cap in the air. "I'm almost ready," I pleaded.

"But I'm a majorette," Michelle protested.

"She's older, so she should stay . . ." My voice slowed down as I noticed my mother's concerned look. Grandpa had been sick and couldn't be left alone today.

"You both will have to decide this now," she said, "or I will decide it for you. I'm due at the hospital." With that she headed off to change her clothes.

Michelle and I stared silently at each other. From the next bedroom we could hear Grandpa's faint snoring. He needs me, I thought. Then I looked at Michelle in her glittering sequins, and I knew how much being in the parade meant to her. "Well," I sighed, "you go. I'll stay home with Grandpa." I let my baseball cap drop to the floor.

Michelle was so excited that she ran out the door and didn't call thanks until she was halfway down the front steps. A few minutes later I heard the door close again as Mother left for the hospital. I picked up a book I had been reading the night before and stretched out across my bed.

I tried to forget about missing the parade, but I could hear faint bits of band music and drumming as I read. Every few minutes someone shot off a firecracker, so I couldn't forget this was the Fourth of July.

Grandpa slept the whole afternoon. I must have fallen asleep, too, for the next thing I knew someone was shaking my shoulder. "Tim, wake up!"

It was Michelle. She was wearing a blue ribbon below her left shoulder. It looked beautiful against the sparkle of the sequins. "I won a prize! I won *first* prize!" she exclaimed. Without pausing for me to say anything, Michelle went on talking, telling me all about the parade and the judging of the marching units.

Just then Grandpa woke up. Michelle and I ran in to tell him about the ribbon. We were in the bedroom talking to Grandpa when Mom returned. She looked a bit tired, but she gave us all a warm smile. She leaned over to kiss Grandpa.

"You know, Pa, I have two wonderful children," she said.

He nodded and reached out to hold my hand and Michelle's. "I knew that all the time," he said.

"And I won a blue ribbon!" Michelle reminded all of us.

"That's wonderful," Mom said, "and I'm proud of you." Then she looked directly at me and went on. "Sometimes there is no ribbon for being a winner. You did something very generous in offering to stay at home, Tim. I was able to prevent a young man from losing his leg. He is a fortunate person today and a very happy one, too." She gave my left shoulder a loving squeeze.

Grandpa winked at me, too.

Good as a Boy

By Jean Richards

"It's just because I'm a girl," Holly said.

"No, Holly, that's not the reason," Mr. Miles answered. "I have already hired all the help I need." The farmer paused. "This morning Mr. Banes told me he was looking for a young fellow to help gather sap. Why not try there?"

Holly felt her face flush hot with annoyance. "You said yourself that he wants a boy."

"Now, Holly, he just said that because most children who want to help with the maple-syrup harvest are boys. Tell Mr. Banes you worked for me last spring vacation, and tell him that I recommend you."

At first Holly's face lit up, but then she sobered again. "The kids call him Cranky Mr. Banes."

Mr. Miles looked at her carefully. "Don't believe everything you hear, Holly. It *is* true that Mr. Banes is a hard worker, and he will expect the same from you if he hires you."

Holly decided there was nothing to do but try. As she turned down the lane, she wondered if Mr. Banes would pay fifteen dollars a day. That was what the boys earned. But maybe he would think a girl would work for less!

Holly found Mr. Banes loading sap buckets on the sled. "What do you want?" He greeted her suspiciously, but Holly would not give in to the impulse to run away.

"Mr. Miles told me you needed someone to help gather maple sap," she told him.

"That's right," said Mr. Banes with a scowl, "but I was thinking of hiring a boy. I don't know . . ."

Holly interrupted. "I know how to tap the trees, set the spouts, and hang the buckets to catch the sap. I worked for Mr. Miles last year, and he said he would recommend me."

Mr. Banes continued to scowl, but then he

shrugged his shoulders. "OK, we'll give it a try. If you give me a good day's work, you'll have the job. Be here at seven Monday morning."

Mr. Banes was already in the maple grove when Holly arrived on Monday morning. Quickly he outlined all he expected of her, which was a lot.

As Holly drilled her first hole in the rough trunk of a huge tree, she realized she had not talked to Mr. Banes about wages. How foolish! But, she reasoned, Mr. Banes must pay the same as the other farmers. She drove the metal spout into the hole and hung a bucket so that the dripping sap would be caught in it. She drove two more taps into the trunk, then moved to the next maple tree.

Soon Mr. Banes came around to inspect what she had done. "From the trees I've tapped already, we'll have enough sap to begin boiling today," he told her.

Later Holly emptied buckets of clear sap into the gathering tank, which was set on a broad sled. When the tank was full, Mr. Banes's horse would pull the sled through the snow to the sugaring shanty. Here the sap would be poured into a gigantic evaporating pan.

Holly watched with interest as Mr. Banes poured the sap. There was a roaring fire under the pan, and soon the sap began to boil. That evening Mr. Banes tested the sap that had boiled down to a thick, golden syrup. He gave Holly a taste, too. It was sweet and delicious.

During the rest of the week Holly helped empty the buckets, boil the sap down to syrup, and put the syrup into containers. Gradually Mr. Banes's frosty attitude thawed, but he still kept praise at a minimum.

Early Saturday morning as Holly walked up to the barn, she heard Mr. Banes talking to his wife. "Holly's a good worker, as good as any boy. Six dollars a day is not too much to offer her."

Holly could not remember when she had ever felt so disappointed. Only six dollars a day! At first she felt like demanding her money and going home, but she forced herself to stay. "Why the long face, Holly?" Mr. Banes asked, noticing that something was wrong.

"It's nothing," Holly said as she bent over her work.

That evening Mr. Banes removed the last of the day's syrup from the pan. "Well, Holly, this is the best sugar crop I've ever had, thanks to your steady work. I'll figure up how much I owe you."

Holly could keep her temper no longer. "Mr. Banes, I worked hard this week. Only six dollars a day for a whole day's work isn't enough."

"Who said anything about six dollars a day? I planned to give you sixteen."

Holly flushed with embarrassment. "But this morning I heard you telling your wife you were going to offer me six dollars."

A broad grin swept over Mr. Banes's face. "Now don't you get so uppity, young lady. I was talking about a steady after-school job. The work here is getting to be too much for me."

Holly hung her head. "I'm sorry, Mr. Banes."

She felt a reassuring hand on her shoulder. "Now, miss, do you want that job or not?"

Holly was quick to tell him she did. As she walked the long way home, she realized that she was going to like getting to know the man that some people called Cranky Mr. Banes.

PENCIL-AND-PAPER CAPER

By Carolyn Crocker

Josh flipped the switch to ON and held his new walkie-talkie to his ear. It hissed, just the way he'd imagined in all those weeks of saving his money.

"*S-s-s-s*. This is Ground Base Zero. On patrol at Mrs. LaVallee's fence. Do you read me? Do you read me?" Rebecca sounded loud and clear.

"Yes, I copy, Chief Inspector," Josh answered from his post behind the garage. But Rebecca was still transmitting.

"Come in, Sarge. Come in, Sarge." She sounded impatient, but until she stopped talking, Josh couldn't get his message through.

"Loud and clear," Josh shouted. The walkie-talkies would be great as soon as they got the hang of them. "Loud and clear. Loud and clear. Over."

"Hey! Let's see how far away we can transmit and still receive," yelled Rebecca. "I'll ride down the street, and you keep talking." Silence. "Oh yeah, over."

"Roger," Josh said, "but put it in your bike basket, OK? The man at the store said they break easily if they get dropped. Or wet. Over."

"I'm not going swimming!" Rebecca hooted. "Oh yeah, over."

Josh kept up a stream of chatter lifted from every police show he'd ever seen. He had just about run out of suspicious activity to report when his walkie-talkie went dead.

He thought at first he might have turned it off by mistake. But the walkie-talkie's switch was still on. He shook it a little. No hiss. He shook it harder. Still no hiss. He had just opened it to check the batteries when Rebecca rode back.

"Hey! How come you didn't answer me? I got all the way down to the One-Stop store, and I could still hear you!" She finally noticed that Josh was less than thrilled. "What's the matter?"

"I don't know," Josh said. "It just quit."

"You didn't try scuba diving with it, did you? Or using it for a soccer ball?"

"Very funny." Josh poked at a red wire and held the set to his ear, hoping for even the faintest hiss. Nothing.

"It couldn't be the batteries already," Rebecca said more seriously. "Well, return it and get your money back if your mom can't fix it."

Josh's mother was famous in the neighborhood for unkinking bike chains and saving cranky toasters from untimely trips to the dump. But even she couldn't tinker a spark of life into the maze of wires and cells of the walkie-talkie.

"I guess we'll have to take it back tomorrow after school."

A different clerk waited on them at the radio store.

"Sorry, sonny," he said, without sounding too sorry. "You have to have a sales slip, or else we can't tell when you bought it. But I'll check the batteries for you." The tester light flashed, as Josh knew it would.

"But, even *with* a sales slip, we would not take a return on that item," he went on, handing the

51

batteries back. "It's just too delicate, and most kids don't know how to handle it." He moved to help some people who were looking at color TVs.

"Come on, Josh," his mother said. "We'll figure out something. It's disappointing to have something break before you've had it twenty-four hours." Her voice rose at the end so that even with his back turned the clerk would hear her. Loud and clear.

On the way home, Josh slumped in the car, flipping the switch on and off, hoping for a miracle.

"It's not fair," he said. "I didn't drop it or get it wet or anything."

"Maybe we can fix it with a pencil and paper," his mother answered. "You didn't throw away the package, did you?"

The package! Josh thought back. He'd been so eager to get his hands on his walkie-talkies that he'd ripped the package to shreds. Then he'd had to piece it together to read the instructions on the back. He'd stashed the bits in the bag, crumpled it all, and stowed it under the seat of the car.

He pulled out the crumpled bag, but he didn't see how it would help.

On the kitchen table, he fitted the package together like a jigsaw puzzle. His mother picked up a piece with print so small it was almost invisible.

"Write our address at the top and copy theirs over here," Josh's mother said as she pointed to the left side of a sheet of paper. "Then write 'Dear Customer Relations Department.' Underneath, tell the company exactly what happened. Ask them to fix your walkie-talkie or send you a new one. Be polite, and don't forget to sign your name."

When he finished, Josh put his letter and the walkie-talkie into a box and took them to the post office.

He had marked off twenty days on his calendar before he found a box waiting for him when he got home from school. Inside was a new walkie-talkie, still in the package, and a letter.

Dear Josh:

Thank you for calling our attention to the defect in unit SX-126. We hope that you will find this new unit satisfactory. Please don't hesitate to contact us if it is not.

Yours sincerely,

Melvin R. Roberts

Customer Relations

Josh carefully pulled the plastic away from the cardboard backing to get out the new set. He added the empty package to his mother's drawer full of warranties and owner's manuals.

The new set worked fine. It didn't need its first battery change for three whole weeks, shortly after Josh discovered that the signal reached Rebecca's house from his. Anytime, day or night. Loud and clear.

Darlene's Dance Dilemma

By Barbara Owen Webb

Darlene made a face at herself in the mirror as she braided her hair before leaving for ballet class. It was awful to feel so mixed up. All her life she had wanted to take ballet lessons, but now that she was taking them, she wasn't so sure. It wasn't that she expected to look like the ballerina she'd seen in Swan Lake, but she had thought dancing would be more fun and less work. It had always looked like fun.

Darlene grabbed her ballet case and hurried down the street to Janice's house. When Janice opened the door, she was munching on an apple. Her dark hair hung loose on her shoulders.

"Come on," said Darlene. "It's time for ballet. How come you haven't got your hair done?"

Janice shrugged. "I'm not going," she said. "I don't think I'm going to take ballet lessons anymore. It's not that fun, and my muscles get sore."

"But you can't stop," protested Darlene. "We started this together. Our mothers paid for the whole twenty-week session."

Janice chewed a piece of apple. "Mom said I didn't have to if I didn't want to."

"Oh," mumbled Darlene. "Well, I'll see you."

Darlene stared at the sidewalk as she walked the three blocks to ballet school. Now she didn't even have her best friend taking classes with her. But how could she tell *her* mother she wanted to quit? After all those years of begging to take dancing lessons, her parents had finally said, "Well, if you really want to." How could she, after two and a half months of classes, say, "I don't want to take ballet lessons anymore. I changed my mind."

As class began, Darlene stood in first position. At least her feet seemed to get into the positions better than when she first started, she thought.

"Darlene, keep your eyes straight ahead," Miss Vronsky commanded.

Darlene stared at the part in the girl's hair in front of her as the students began their *pliés*.

"No, no," Miss Vronsky said, taking the needle off the record. "I know it's difficult, boys and girls. But you must not let your bodies be lazy. It is like this: when you are at home, your parents tell you to do chores and you do them. Now you are like parents telling your legs and arms and feet to work. You must tell your bodies what to do and not let them be lazy."

Darlene thought that was kind of silly. Imagine saying to your back, "All right now, back, you'd better straighten up." She tried hard not to giggle out loud at the thought.

By the time she got home after class, Darlene wondered if maybe there was some way she could tell her mother that she wanted to quit taking ballet.

"Hi, honey," said Mom as Darlene opened the door. "Did you have a good class?"

Darlene put down her ballet case. "Janice isn't taking lessons anymore," she said, avoiding her mother's question.

"Is she sick or something?" Mom sounded surprised.

"No, she just doesn't like it," Darlene said, watching her mother's expression.

"After her parents paid for the whole session? I don't see how she can get away with that."

"Well, I'd better go shower, I guess," said Darlene. She could see her mother's opinion of quitting ballet. Maybe she'd wait until she finished this session, before the next session was paid for. Then she'd just tell her parents she had been wrong about wanting to take ballet, that she was sorry she'd nagged them so much, and that she wanted to stop. That's what she'd do.

The next-to-last lesson came in January. Miss Vronsky gave the command for *grands battements*. Some of the students groaned. It was one of those steps that look easy, but are just plain hard.

Well, thought Darlene, I'm going to get it right today. Inside her head she talked to her body. She felt silly, but she tried it anyway.

"All right now, head, keep erect; knees, don't you dare bend; in, stomach, keep in, that's the way," she said to her body as she did the *grands battements*.

"Why, Darlene," Miss Vronsky said as the music finished, "that was well done. Here's a girl who's making her body work; I can see it." Darlene blinked and stared at her teacher. Miss Vronsky smiled. "Please take the *barre* and demonstrate the step for everyone, Darlene."

Darlene could feel her face getting hot. At the front of the room she rested her hand lightly on the *barre* and faced the mirror. Again she talked to her legs and stomach, but her attention was drawn to herself in the mirror. She looked . . . well, she looked good! Her body was erect. Her legs were straight. She smiled at herself and somehow *grands battements* even felt good.

On the way home after class, Darlene met Janice on the sidewalk.

"How was ballet?" Janice asked.

"It was fun today," Darlene said. "Miss Vronsky said I'm getting better." Suddenly she added, "Wait till you see me in the recital in June. You'll really be surprised."

But no one was more surprised than Darlene that at last ballet was fun.

ROBERTO GETS THROUGH AUGUST

By Katherine Nye Rolfes

"August is a useless month," Roberto said as he tossed the July calendar page into the trash. "There's nothing at all to look forward to."

"It isn't so bad," his mother said. "At least we don't have to worry about icy streets."

"But there's nothing to do," Roberto complained. "There isn't one holiday to look forward to, either."

August didn't give Roberto a single reason to make decorations or, perhaps, a special card for his mother.

"Better make the best of it," his mother said as she kissed him good-bye. "School will be here before you know it!"

Roberto liked school. He liked being with his friends and learning about how things worked. "School is better than having nothing to do," Roberto said with a sigh.

After his mother left for work, Roberto helped himself to another bowl of cereal. Then he watched a rerun he had seen a month ago. What a waste of time, Roberto thought unhappily. He cleaned up the breakfast things and locked the apartment door behind him.

People on the street bumped elbows as they hurried toward jobs and appointments. No one smiled. That's because it's so hot and miserable, Roberto decided. When there's something to look forward to, people are friendly, he thought.

Hot gusts of wind gathered up the litter from the gutter and whirled it around Roberto's knees. Exhaust fumes from the traffic blended with the wavy heat above the street. August is an awful month, Roberto thought.

"Hi, Roberto!" Miss Jules said when Roberto got to the bookmobile. "Hot enough for you today?"

"Yes," Roberto mumbled. "Maybe a book about the ocean will help me feel cooler."

Roberto had been to the ocean once when he was very small. He remembered how nice the cool mist and waves had felt. He thought of the way the sunlight had bounced off the glistening water.

"Look over there on the bottom shelf," Miss Jules instructed. "The ocean picture book should be there."

Roberto looked all along the bottom row. There were books about dolphins and dragons and pandas. But there was no book about the ocean.

"Maybe someone has checked it out," Roberto suggested.

"No, I don't think so," said Miss Jules. "My records show that the book should be here."

Miss Jules looked along the bottom shelf. Then she looked in the box marked "Returns." The ocean book was gone.

"I guess I haven't been keeping very good records," she said with a sigh. "There doesn't seem to be enough time. Perhaps I can straighten it out later on."

Outside, small boys and girls had gathered on the steps of the nearby apartment building. Mothers fanned themselves with folded papers. Babies squirmed in their strollers. "Is everyone ready for story time?" Miss Jules asked, smiling.

"Yes!" the children shouted.

Roberto liked listening to the story. He liked watching the children's faces as they listened. He could almost see the wheels clicking in their minds as they wondered about the pictures.

When story time was over, Roberto followed Miss Jules back into the bookmobile. "I like to read, Miss Jules," he said. "Could I help you once in a while by reading for story time?"

Miss Jules thought for a moment. "That would give me time to sort out the books and get the files caught up," she said.

"I could come as often as you like," Roberto smiled. "I don't have anything else to do."

"All right, Roberto!" Miss Jules said. "Why don't you come back this afternoon after lunch? You may choose several of your favorite stories to read aloud."

Roberto waited until every spot on the steps was filled before he began to read. He held the book about clowns up high so all of the boys and girls could see the pictures. "Roberto's a good reader," whispered one little girl.

"I like the way he shows the pictures, too," said another child.

When the stories were finished, the children applauded. "Hooray for Roberto!" they cheered.

Roberto felt proud. He was glad he had found something useful to do. He couldn't wait to tell his mother. I'll surprise her, he thought.

On his way home Roberto stopped at the store. He bought a package of vividly colored construction paper and two red balloons. When he got home, he cut yellow flowers from the paper and taped them to the wall. Then he blew up the balloons and hung them from the knob on the cupboard. He made a special card for his mother and set the table for dinner.

"Surprise!" Roberto called when his mother came in. "We're going to celebrate!"

"What's all this?" his mother asked.

"I found something useful to do today!" Roberto explained. "I'm going to read stories every day at the bookmobile to help Miss Jules."

"Roberto! That's wonderful!" his mother said. She gave him a big hug.

"Now I'll have something to look forward to each day," Roberto said.

When supper was finished, Roberto used a sharp red pencil to write "STORY TIME" on the August page of the calendar. "August isn't such a bad month after all!" he said, grinning.

What If?

By Carolyn Luetje

Mary Melissa Matthews liked to ask "what if?" Sometimes her questions were quite silly, such as "What if we all turned blue?" Sometimes her questions were quite sensible, such as "What if someone got hurt and there was no one around to help?" And sometimes her questions were just plain outrageous, such as "What if a spaceship full of Martians landed in our yard?"

Mother and Father usually answered Mary Melissa's questions. "We'd just have to get new family photos taken," they replied when she asked about turning blue. "Go to the nearest telephone and call the emergency number," they advised when she asked about someone getting hurt. But when she asked about the Martians in the backyard, they declared, "Mary Melissa Matthews, that's enough—no more questions for today!" Then Mary Melissa knew it was time to stop what-iffing!

Every Thursday Mrs. Matthews went into the city to work at the hospital. After school on Thursdays Mary Melissa rode the school bus out into the country and got off at Grandma's house. She and Grandma baked cookies and read books, and sometimes they walked down the road to Johnson's Grocery Store. Late in the afternoon Mr. and Mrs. Matthews would come by to pick up Mary Melissa on their way home from the city. Thursday was Mary Melissa's favorite day of the week.

One Thursday afternoon Mary Melissa spent the whole bus ride wondering "what if?" "What if the bears slept all winter but forgot to wake up in the spring?" she wondered to herself. "What if the trees lost all their leaves and new ones never grew again?" she thought. "What if all the kids came to school but the teacher thought it was Sunday?" She giggled when she thought about having school without a teacher. Just then she looked out the window and saw Grandma's house up ahead. "What if I forgot to get off the bus at Grandma's house?" she wondered as she hopped off the bus.

Mary Melissa skipped up Grandma's front walk and rang the doorbell. When no one came to the door, she rang the bell again. "What if nobody is home?" she wondered. She knocked on the door. Then she knocked again, harder.

She walked around to the back of the house. "Maybe Grandma is hanging laundry on the clothesline," she thought. But Grandma wasn't there.

Mary Melissa went back to the front door and rang the doorbell again. She peeked through the front window, but she didn't see Grandma anywhere. She knocked again, harder and longer. "What if Grandma's hurt and can't come to the door?" she thought to herself.

Suddenly Mary Melissa knew just what to do. "Call the emergency number," Mother and Father had said when she had asked about someone getting hurt.

Mary Melissa ran down the road to the pay telephone outside Johnson's Grocery Store and began to dial.

Even before Mary Melissa got back to Grandma's house, she could hear the sirens off in the distance. She began to worry. "What if Grandma just didn't hear me knocking?" she thought. "What if she was on the phone and couldn't come to the door?"

The sirens came closer and closer. "What if Grandma thought today was Wednesday and she went shopping in the city instead?" she worried.

By the time the emergency crew arrived, Mary Melissa was very upset. "I . . . I . . . ," she stammered. "I always come on Thursdays, but Grandma didn't answer the door," she blurted out. "Maybe she's hurt!"

One of the crew members ran up the sidewalk to Grandma's front door. He broke the window, then reached inside and turned the doorknob.

"Oh, no!" Mary Melissa whispered to herself as the glass shattered. "What if Grandma's just out behind the barn working in her garden? What if I made a *terrible* mistake?"

The emergency workers rushed into Grandma's house. Mary Melissa went inside, too, and listened. She thought she heard Grandma calling her.

"This way," Mary Melissa said. "I think Grandma's back here."

"Mary Melissa! Mary Melissa!" She could hear Grandma's voice louder now. She opened the bedroom door and saw Grandma lying on the floor.

"Oh, Grandma!" she exclaimed. "What happened?"

"I was standing on a chair, trying to change a light bulb," Grandma explained. "I lost my balance and fell. I think I broke my leg. Thank goodness it's Thursday. I knew you'd come."

Soon Grandma was placed on a stretcher and carried out to the ambulance. Mr. and Mrs. Matthews arrived just as the ambulance was ready to take Grandma to the hospital.

The ambulance driver told Mary Melissa's mother and father what had happened. "You should be very proud of your daughter," she said. "She knew just what to do in an emergency."

Mary Melissa smiled quietly, but she didn't say anything. In fact, she was very quiet that evening.

The next morning at breakfast Mary Melissa began what-iffing again. "What if people walked on their hands instead of their feet? What if we turned on the faucet and lemonade came out instead of water? What if—"

"Mary Melissa, I'm sure you'll always know just what to do, no matter what happens," Mother interrupted.

"Yes," Father agreed, "you certainly will."

But Mother and Father never told Mary Melissa to stop what-iffing again.

The Snowman on Sled Hill

By Pat Rugh Mahan

The snow stopped falling early Saturday morning. At 120 Maple Street Ted thought breakfast would take forever. By the time he and his sister, Cassie, burst out the front door, they could already hear excited shouts from the park a block away.

"Ted, look! The snow is up to my knees!" Cassie giggled as she fell into the soft whiteness. "I can't move!"

"Sure you can. Here, I'll help you." Ted grinned and gave his younger sister a push. She caught his sleeve and pulled him into the snowdrift beside her. Snow flew for a minute until they both sat up, red-cheeked and gasping.

"Hey, Ted!" called a voice from the yard next door.

"Pete," shouted Ted, "come on over!"

"Wait till you hear this." Pete pushed through the snow quickly. "There's a snowman contest at the park! Real prizes, too." Pete brushed some snow out of his dark hair.

"When?" asked Ted.

"Today," Pete answered. "Judging's at noon."

Cassie watched as Ted scooped up a handful of snow and experimentally closed his mittened fingers around it. He opened his hand, and the well-packed snow dropped to the ground with a soft thud.

The two boys grinned. "Let's go!" shouted Pete.

Ted glanced at Cassie. "You can come, too," he said over his shoulder. "You can help us."

Cassie opened her mouth to answer, but the boys had started off. She sighed. If only she, too, had a friend next door! She hurried to catch up.

The park was already crowded. Pete, Ted, and Cassie moved to an open area on the far side and got to work.

Very soon they had a sizable snowman, with

pinecone eyes, a stone nose, and a holly berry mouth.

"He needs a hat. How about yours?" asked Pete. "We don't have time to go home for anything."

"OK," Ted answered, and pulled his wool cap over the snowman's head.

The three stepped back to admire their creation.

"Look out!" shouted a voice. A flash of red was careening down the hill straight toward them!

Whump!

Cassie slowly uncovered her eyes. Their beautiful snowman was once more three uneven balls of snow. A sled lay on its side, and a boy in a red jacket was carefully getting to his feet.

"Don't you know this is the new sled run?" the boy asked. "What are you doing here?"

"Trying to win a contest," Ted answered glumly.

"The snowman contest," Pete added. He pointed to the other side of the park, where two judges had already stopped in front of the first finished snow figure.

Another sled whizzed by.

"Look, you can't stay here," said the boy in the red jacket. "Use my sled, and move your snowman over near that tree." Working in pairs, they hoisted the balls of snow onto the sled and headed for the tall pine.

They were nearly there when Cassie felt the sled jerk and then tip over, stopped by an old stump they hadn't seen. The balls of snow were once more on the ground. This time they lay neatly together, with Ted's knit cap covering the snowman's face.

"Oh, no," groaned Pete and Ted together.

Cassie heard footsteps and looked up.

"And what have we here?" one of the judges asked.

Cassie gave the overturned sled a disappointed kick. "I guess our snowman got tired of sledding and just fell asleep," she said.

The judges looked at each other. Then one of them put his fingers to his lips. "Shh . . . ," he said. The other placed a shiny ribbon on the sleeping snowman. The ribbon read "Honorable Mention for the Most Original Snowman on Sled Hill."

Flipparoos and Walmonks

By Lory Herbison Frame

My friend Professor Goodbody came over to look at my painting. "The cottontail rabbits are too large," he remarked helpfully.

"Those are supposed to be white-tailed deer."

"The goat in the bushes is charming, though," he said, trying to make amends.

"Anyone can see," I said with dignity, "that it's a mountain lion." I pretended to throw my paint-brush at him.

"What are the rab . . . I mean the deer doing?"

"Eating leaves."

"And what is the lion doing?"

"Thinking of eating one of the deer."

"Ah." Dr. Goodbody stared dreamily at the canvas. Slyly, I repaired the deer's ears, trying to make them look less like bunnies.

"Why don't you paint an Australian scene?" he suggested.

"I'd have to start all over."

"No, you wouldn't. All you have to do is paint out the rab . . . er, deer, and put in kangaroos."

"I like the deer," I said stubbornly. "Besides, I want something to be there to eat the grass."

"Kangaroos will eat the grass. You won't miss the deer. Kangaroos are just deer that hop and have pockets."

"Professor, are you feeling all right?"

"Kangaroos are the *ecological equivalent* of the deer. They do the same kind of job. They eat grass. But they do it in Australia."

He had done it again: smuggled a new scientific term into my brain when I wasn't looking!

"I'm not sure I know what 'ecological equivalent' means," I told him.

"It's a simple idea, really," the professor said. "Don't let the long words fool you. An ecological equivalent is an animal that eats the same kind of food as another species of animal living in another place. Because kangaroos and deer both eat leafy plants, they are equivalents. But they live on different continents. It's the same with meat-eaters. There is an ecological equivalent on each of the continents."

"But what," I asked, "are you going to do about an ecological equivalent in Australia of the North American mountain lion?" Now I thought I was very clever, because there is no species of big cat in Australia, none at all.

"A big meat-eater, something to do the mountain lion's job . . . ," he mused. "In Asia we would put in a tiger. If it were Africa . . . a leopard or a cheetah would do nicely. South America . . . a jaguar. Now, in Australia, the only big predator is the dingo, Australia's wild dog. We'll have to switch from the cat to the dog family."

"That's cheating."

"Not at all. Dingoes do the same job as mountain lions do. They eat meat."

"Dingoes often hunt in packs," I said, pointing to my solitary North American mountain lion.

"Change the lion to a pack of North American wolves, then." He got that dreamy look in his eyes again. "Dingoes are just little wolves painted light golden brown. South American bush dogs are just dingoes with short legs. African hunting dogs are just long-legged bush dogs with black-and-white color added to their fur."

"I suppose they all have an ecological equivalent that lives in the sea?" Hah, I thought, let's see him come up with some kind of dog that paddles about in the ocean.

"Of course. Killer whales."

Well, dash it, I should have remembered. Killer whales are pack hunters. They are cunning and fast, and they eat just about anything, including porpoises, seals, sea otters, sharks, walruses, and even an occasional polar bear. And now it came back to me. I had even heard them called the Wolves of the Sea! So that's what it meant!

"Killer whales are just . . ."

"I know, I know." I raised a hand to stop him. "Killer whales are just wolves that look like fish. I would like to get back to my painting now."

"Australia?"

"No, a make-believe place. A new continent full of animals nobody ever saw. Wait till I put in the plants first." And I slapped on large amounts of green paint. "Ready for the plant-eaters."

"I'm thinking of an animal," Dr. Goodbody thought out loud, "that often goes swimming."

I gave the creature flat, webbed feet, so it could

paddle in the water.

"It has short legs, but it has to be able to reach high leaves."

So I gave it a long neck.

"Predators try to sneak up on it."

I gave it large ears so it could hear things sneaking up on it, and I added protective quills. And a white tail.

"Why, it's a flippered, white-tailed kangaroo with prickles! Let's call it the cotton-tailed, prickled flipparoo!"

"Now we need something to eat the flipparoo, the ecological equivalent of the dingoes." I readied my paintbrush.

"I'm thinking of an animal," Dr. Goodbody said, "that has no legs."

I didn't know what to do with the creature for now except to drape it in a tree. I gave it a prehensile (grasping) tail to hang on with.

"It chases flipparoos."

"It would need wings, then." I decided to make them blue.

"It's a small animal, compared to the flipparoo."

So I made a whole pack of them. They would have to work as a team. I added long teeth and scales (to protect against the prickles). They looked like tiny, flying walruses with monkeys' tails.

"Save me! It's the dreaded blue-winged, armor-plated walmonk!" We shrieked with laughter.

"What else?" I flourished my brush.

"I'm thinking of an animal that lives underwater, deep in the sea . . ."

The two of us spent the whole afternoon inventing the most delightfully absurd creatures. All were ecological equivalents of something real, but we made them up in our imaginations. Flipparoos and walmonks indeed!

Who's Afraid of Mr. Sweeney?

By Betsy Sueltenfuss

Every Saturday Luke carried groceries for Mrs. Feldon, his next-door neighbor. Mrs. Feldon paid him to bring the groceries from the store. Luke was saving to buy a new backpack for a camping trip in the mountains.

One Saturday Mrs. Feldon sat at her kitchen table, with her metal walker standing next to her chair. She watched as Luke carefully arranged canned goods in the pantry.

"That's good work, Luke," Mrs. Feldon praised. "I hate to have my vegetable soup lost behind the chicken noodle. I can't stand up for very long to look for things."

She patted the walker next to her. "Not even with the help of Thunder here." She laughed.

"Has Thunder had his oats yet?" Luke asked. "A trusty horse has to be well fed, you know." They both laughed at their old familiar joke.

"He finished grazing right before you got here," Mrs. Feldon teased. Then she winked at Luke. "I'm hungry, though," she said, opening a box of dough-nuts as Luke put away the last of the groceries.

"I'll miss you while you're gone, Luke," she said, her eyes still twinkling over the silly joking.

Between bites of his doughnut, Luke said, "I'll tell you all about the Sierras when I come back." He knew Mrs. Feldon liked to hear his stories. One time she told him he would have to be her eyes as well as her legs.

"Of course you will. Every detail. Then I will feel as if I'd been on vacation, too," Mrs. Feldon said, laughing.

Sometimes Luke was surprised by Mrs. Feldon's laughter. He thought that if he couldn't play Little League baseball or hike with his dad, he wouldn't feel like laughing.

Not Mrs. Feldon! She told corny jokes. She laughed on the phone talking with her friends. She sat on her porch, laughing with the neighbor kids who played keep-away in her yard.

One afternoon Luke and his friends were playing football at Kevin's house. Luke's pass went too far, and the ball sailed right through a neighbor's window. There was a loud crash.

"Uh-oh," Kevin gasped, "that's Mr. Sweeney's house! You broke his window."

Luke had trouble talking. Finally he said weakly, "I'll have to go tell him."

Before he reached the front door, Mr. Sweeney came storming out. "Hey, you!" he screamed, waving a fist in the air. "You'll pay for this!"

"I threw the ball," Luke admitted. "But I'll pay for it," he added, somewhat uncertainly. He thought of the money he had been saving for so long to buy a backpack.

"You bet you will," snapped Mr. Sweeney.

As Luke was telling his parents what had happened, he said, "Kevin says Mr. Sweeney has been in the hospital. But I don't care if he *is* sick, he still shouldn't be so mean."

Later Mrs. Feldon told him that Mr. Sweeney had been sick for years. "He has an illness that makes it hard for him to breathe," she explained.

"But you never get mean," Luke said, "when your legs hurt."

Mrs. Feldon smiled, but she shook her head thoughtfully. "Oh, but sometimes I'm not in the best of moods either."

Luke's father went with him to pay for the window. Luke was glad for the company, but his dad made him do most of the talking. "I'm sure sorry, Mr. Sweeney," Luke apologized.

Mr. Sweeney frowned and waggled a finger. "Sorry never takes the place of careful," he scolded.

It wasn't long before Luke forgot about Mr. Sweeney. It was time for the Sierra Nevada trip Luke carefully arranged everything in his old backpack. It was small and one of the pockets was ripped, but it would have to do.

Luke and his dad were gone for a week. They hiked, fished, and slept in a tent. When they returned, Luke found out that Mrs. Feldon had been very sick.

When he went next door to see her, she was in her bed. A friend was taking care of her.

"I'm sorry, Luke," Mrs. Feldon whispered. "I don't feel up to company right now."

Luke tried again the next day, but Mrs. Feldon's friend shook her head. "She doesn't feel like talking to anyone," she said.

Luke wanted to say, "Not even me?" He felt hurt and even a little angry.

On Saturday he delivered Mrs. Feldon's groceries as usual. Her friend hadn't come yet. Luke stood at the bedroom doorway and called softly, "Hello." He felt sure Mrs. Feldon would be ready for his visit this time.

"Put them anywhere," Mrs. Feldon said in a harsh voice. "Lucille will put them away later." Luke didn't even get a chance to ask if he could come in. "Don't let the kitchen door slam when you leave," Mrs. Feldon added sharply.

It was several weeks before Mrs. Feldon got better. One day Luke was surprised to see her in the kitchen when he came with the groceries. He was even more surprised to see that she was in a wheelchair.

"Thunder is resting at the stable," she said with a grin. She tapped the arm of her wheelchair. "Meet Star—my new horse."

Luke was happy to see Mrs. Feldon laughing and joking again.

"Now sit right here," she ordered, pointing toward a chair. "I simply can't wait another minute to hear about The Great Sierra Adventure."

A few days later Luke was playing hide-and-seek in Kevin's front yard. Luke was hiding behind an ivy-covered trellis when he heard a voice. "Hey, you. Come over here."

Luke gulped. It was Mr. Sweeney. The trellis was in Kevin's yard, so what could Mr. Sweeney be upset about?

"Come here," he repeated, motioning to Luke.

Luke walked hesitantly up to the door.

"I hear you are Mrs. Feldon's good friend," Mr. Sweeney said. "You help her out and visit her?"

Luke nodded.

"She's a friend of mine, too."

Luke was surprised to see Mr. Sweeney smile. At least he thought it was a smile—it was just a small one. And Mr. Sweeney's voice seemed softer than before. "Can you come inside?" he asked. "Won't take long."

In the hallway Mr. Sweeney handed Luke a large box. "This is for you."

Luke couldn't believe his eyes and ears. Was it some kind of joke?

He pulled the paper off the box and opened it. "An alpine backpack!" He looked up at Mr. Sweeney. "How did you know?"

"Mrs. Feldon told me you were saving your money for it. I hope I got the right one."

"It's the one, all right," Luke nodded. "But why would you give me a gift?"

Mr. Sweeney cleared his throat. His eyes suddenly grew misty. "Well . . . to apologize, I guess." He coughed nervously. "You didn't throw that ball through my window on purpose. Guess I forgot what it was like to be a kid. I haven't been one for a good while, you know."

"But you didn't have to—"

"Go on now," Mr. Sweeney interrupted. "You've stayed long enough." His voice was gruff again.

This time Luke wasn't frightened by Mr. Sweeney's rough ways. He thought about how different Mrs. Feldon had acted when she was sick. Maybe it *was* just Mr. Sweeney's illness that made him act grumpy sometimes.

Luke started off to find Kevin. He couldn't wait to show him the backpack. But he remembered to stop on the sidewalk and shout back, "Thanks. Thanks a lot."

Mr. Sweeney was just closing his front door. Luke wasn't sure if Mr. Sweeney had heard him calling. "Maybe I'll go back someday to thank him again," Luke told himself. Then he thought, "I wonder if Mr. Sweeney would like to hear about The Great Sierra Adventure?"

Too Many Jennifers

By Kathy Balestrini

There were too many Jennifers in the world, and I was one of them!

There were three Jennifers in Super Electric Room Eleven, my class. Jennifer C. and Jennifer S. and me, Jennifer M.

Confusing, but I was used to it. Then a new Jennifer moved in right on my block.

I first saw this Jennifer one day after school.

"Jennifer!" a woman called from the yellow house. I looked around. Was she calling me?

"Jennifer! Come have some Yummie Nibbles."

And the new Jennifer came running across the yard. She had reddish hair—kind of shaggy—and big brown eyes and . . . a floppy tail. The new Jennifer was a dog! I had to do something.

"Change your name?" my mother said.

I nodded. "I'll think of a special name." I took my homework to my room. When I finished my math, I made a list of names—Erin, Jessica, Tracy, Melissa. But there were girls in my class with those names.

After I did my spelling, I wrote a list of names that nobody in my class had. I put down my mother's name, Linda, and then Judy, Denise, Carol. Not for me.

I needed a break in the middle of social studies, so I thought of names from my grandmother's day. Helen, Rose, Ethel. Not me.

After I had listed the last state capital, I still hadn't found a name, so I thought of my favorite things. Books, pizza, soccer. No, Pizza M. wasn't what I had in mind. I looked around my room at all my pictures. An idea came to me in a flash!

Rainbow! I love rainbows, and I had rainbow pictures everywhere. "I thought of a name," I told Mom. "It's my favorite thing."

"Pizza?"

"Oh, Mom. It's Rainbow!"

"Rainbow?" she said. "It reminds me of your sixth birthday."

"When a clown came?" I said. "Oh. Rainbow the Clown. I don't think I want a clown's name."

I went back and looked around my room again. I had fixed it up with my favorite things and helped paint it my favorite color.

All of a sudden I knew my new name.

"Lavender?" Mom said. "I like it!"

"Lavender?" Mr. Lee said the next day at school. He took off his glasses. "Not Jennifer M. anymore?"

I shook my head. "Now there will be only two Jennifers in Super Electric Room Eleven. It will be a lot less confusing."

"Definitely." Mr. Lee wrote Lavender above Jennifer M. in his grade book. It took a week or two, but finally everybody got used to calling me Lavender.

I don't know when I started to get tired of my new name. Maybe on my birthday when all my presents were lavender. Lavender pajamas and lavender barrettes. Lavender socks and lavender soap. I was hoping for books and games, but they don't usually come in lavender.

The next day Mr. Lee assigned an art project, to make a poster that showed who we were.

"Just write our names on it?" Danny asked.

"If you are only a name," Mr. Lee said. "But I think all of you are much more than that. Show the things that make you who you are."

Easy, I thought. After school I stirred blue paint into pink until it turned just the right shade of lavender. Then I painted one side of a poster board until it was all lavender. That's me, I thought.

All week long I listened to everybody talk about the posters they were making. I didn't tell anybody about mine.

Then, the day before the art assignment was due, Mr. Lee told us to be ready to give a talk about our posters.

What was I going to say? "Lavender. That's me. And that's all."

When I got home from school, I looked at my poster for a long time. Then I took a deep breath. Lavender was pretty, but I was more than just a color. I was more than just a name. I turned the board over and got to work.

When it was my turn on poster day, I held up the lavender side.

"This is me," I said. "Lavender. It's a color I like, and it's a name I like."

Then I turned the poster over so the class could see the new side.

"This is also me." I pointed at the pictures I had taped on. "I like soccer and rainbows and pizza. I like all kinds of animals. I like Super Electric Room Eleven, so I put in our class picture."

Everybody laughed, especially Mr. Lee.

"And there's something else that my poster shows about me. Sometimes I feel one way, and sometimes I feel another way."

I showed the lavender side again. "For a while I wanted my name to be Lavender." I flipped the poster back. "But now I'd like to be Jennifer M. again."

I stood my poster next to the others, with the Jennifer side out. Everybody clapped. I was so embarrassed I turned . . . pink!"

That afternoon I stopped to talk to the new Jennifer on the block. Since I like animals, I thought I ought to get to know her.

"I'm Jennifer M.," I told her. "And I'll call you Jennifer D. You know, D as in Dog. Just so we don't get confused."